ALEX

and

THE OTHER

Other Weird Stories Gone Wrong:

Jake and the Giant Hand
Myles and the Monster Outside
Carter and the Curious Maze

WEIRD STORIES GONE WRONG

ALEX

and

THE OTHER

PHILIPPA DOWDING

Illustrations by Shawna Daigle

DUNDURN

TORONTO

Cover image: Shawna Daigle
Printer: Webcom

Library and Archives Canada Cataloguing in Publication

Dowding, Philippa, 1963-, author
    Alex and the other / Philippa Dowding.

(Weird stories gone wrong)
Issued print and electronic formats.
ISBN 978-1-4597-4063-1 (softcover).--ISBN 978-1-4597-4064-8 (PDF).--ISBN 978-1-4597-4065-5 (EPUB)

I. Title. II. Series: Dowding, Philippa, 1963- . Weird stories gone wrong

PS8607.O9874A44 2018   jC813'.6   C2017-904951-8
                                             C2017-904952-6

1 2 3 4 5   22 21 20 19 18

 Conseil des Arts du Canada   Canada Council for the Arts    Canada    ONTARIO ARTS COUNCIL CONSEIL DES ARTS DE L'ONTARIO an Ontario government agency un organisme du gouvernement de l'Ontario

We acknowledge the support of the **Canada Council for the Arts**, which last year invested $153 million to bring the arts to Canadians throughout the country, and the **Ontario Arts Council** for our publishing program. We also acknowledge the financial support of the **Government of Ontario**, through the **Ontario Book Publishing Tax Credit** and the **Ontario Media Development Corporation**, and the **Government of Canada**.

Nous remercions le **Conseil des arts du Canada** de son soutien. L'an dernier, le Conseil a investi 153 millions de dollars pour mettre de l'art dans la vie des Canadiennes et des Canadiens de tout le pays.

Care has been taken to trace the ownership of copyright material used in this book. The author and the publisher welcome any information enabling them to rectify any references or credits in subsequent editions.

— *J. Kirk Howard, President*

The publisher is not responsible for websites or their content unless they are owned by the publisher.

Printed and bound in Canada.

VISIT US AT

🌐 dundurn.com | 🐦 @dundurnpress | f dundurnpress | 📷 dundurnpress

Dundurn
3 Church Street, Suite 500
Toronto, Ontario, Canada
M5E 1M2

For Allister

THIS PART IS (MOSTLY) TRUE

You should know, before you even start this book, that it's a little scary. And parts of it are even a bit weird and strange. I wish I could make the story less scary and strange, but this is the way I heard it, so I really have no choice.

It starts like this:

A long time ago, an old farmer woke in the middle of the night, to the sound of his pigs.

They were screaming out in the pigpen.

Now, if you've never heard a pig scream, you're lucky. They sound like, well "other-worldly," might be the best word for what they sound like. It makes your hair stand up.

The old farmer looked out his bedroom window, and the pigs were going crazy. The piglets rammed into the fence again and again, and their mother, the old sow, tried to dig her way out of the pigpen (something that had never occurred to her before).

"Darn coyotes again," the old farmer said. The pigs never liked coyotes. With good reason.

The old farmer grabbed his boots and ran into the winter night. He burst out the kitchen door, tramped across the crunchy snow …

… and stopped dead.

His pigs fell silent. They stood perfectly still and looked at him. Which was a bit unnerving.

A strange green fog swirled around them, like a swamp gas or a mysterious vapour. The moon was up and shone on the snow and on the pigs staring at the farmer.

"What the …?" The old farmer moved closer to get a better look and stopped again. At the edge of the green fog, two tall strangers in long overcoats stood beside the fence. Definitely *not* coyotes.

The strangers stood perfectly still. And watched him.

Just like the pigs.

The silent pigs and the tall figures stared at him in the eerie green fog and the moonlit silence. The farmer suddenly felt very exposed.

"Who are you? What are you doing to my pigs?" he called out. The weird fog swirled, and a green finger of fog stretched toward him.

There was no answer. He called again. "What do you want with my pigs?"

The wind blew, the green fog stretched across the ground toward him …

… and a strange voice answered, *"We seek The Other."*

The old farmer swallowed hard. The voice! The voice was nothing like he'd ever heard before. A squeal. A rasp. A grunt. It made his hair stand up.

"What's that? What's *The Other*? What do you mean?" He tried to get a better look at the tall strangers, but they were shrouded in the green fog. The pigs turned and looked at the strangers as though they were waiting for an answer, too.

"Beware The Other," the awful voice said. It sounded … *exactly* … like a pig might if it decided to start talking to you. The farmer swallowed again.

"Who are you?" he called.

But as he watched, the strangers turned and vanished into the foggy trees.

Every piggy eye in the pigpen turned to look at the old farmer. A distinctly piggy voice said, "They'll be back."

Which was when the farmer turned, ran back into the house, and jumped under his bed. It took his wife a long time to coax him out. The next day a FOR SALE sign was on the farm and the old farmer never, ever spoke about that night again, not to anyone. The pigs were sold to a farmer down the lane. The odd thing was (although, really, what part of this story *isn't* odd?), when it came time to count and sell them, there were two piglets missing. And then there weren't. A little while later, they turned up again.

Who ever heard of a weird green fog that made pigs panic? Or vanish and reappear? Or *talk*, for that matter?

But every once in a while, in that time and place, a strange story popped up about a green fog that swirled across a winter barn-yard and panicked the pigs. The story usually included a missing pig or two and mysterious, tall strangers looking for something, but no one was quite sure what it was.

It's weird, I know, but as you've likely heard somewhere, sometimes truth can be stranger than fiction. Which you're about to find out.

You don't have to believe this story. But just because things are odd or a little strange or unbelievable doesn't always make them untrue. Truth is an odd thing; one person's truth can be another person's lie. That's the most important thing to remember about this story: sometimes things that seem like lies are actually true. And sometimes you never can tell.

That's the spookiest thing of all.

CHAPTER 1

IT STARTS WITH A WINK

The hallway was dark and smelled like the boiler room and fresh oil paint.

Technically, Alex wasn't supposed to be down there.

Technically.

But it was his favourite place in school at lunchtime, because it was quiet and dark. No one ever went down there except the old janitor. And even if he did, he never noticed Alex.

Because no one ever did.

No, the technically off-limits boy's bathroom in the basement of Rosewood Public

School was the perfect place to hide out at lunchtime. And Alex was good at hiding.

He was so good at hiding, he was practically invisible.

He slipped quietly past all the kids going for lunch. He snuck down the basement stairs and along the marble floor, past the boiler room. He passed the storage rooms full of buckets and mops and disinfectant and walked to the end of the dark hall. He opened the door.

And sighed.

The boy's bathroom *was* empty, as always. Just the way Alex liked it.

Why was it empty?

Because it was *haunted*.

Or at least the *mirror* in the boy's bathroom was, or so the story went. What public school *doesn't* have the legend of a haunted bathroom mirror in the creepy, darkest place in the basement? Some boy was supposed to have vanished into the mirror the year the school was built, back in the 1930s. He went in to wash his hands and never came out.

Except now and then he popped up in the mirror, crying for help. Or so say the kids who claim to have seen him. But Alex never had and didn't expect to because he didn't believe that kind of thing.

And the haunted mirror story wasn't really why the bathroom was closed. Nothing worked in the bathroom and hadn't for years.

Alex settled on the floor and took his lunch out of his backpack. He leaned against the wall and stared at the ceiling. It was silent, and he was alone. Just the way he liked it.

Another six weeks.

His parents were gone to Australia for six weeks. Again. Except last time it was Egypt. And before that it was Nepal. And before that … he forgot where they went before that.

And the only person he had to take care of him was his older brother, Carl. Not that there was anything wrong with Carl, exactly. It was just he was so much older and didn't even live with Alex. He only stayed at the farm when their parents were away. Plus he worked all day and hardly knew his little brother.

Carl also whistled. All. Day. Long.

The only real friend Alex had was his cat, Needles.

Alex chewed his sandwich. A snowball banged against the outside of the frosted bathroom window at ground level above him.

Boots ran past the glass, and he heard kids shout at each other in the snowy field in the world above and outside.

He finished his soup. When he stood up to leave, he looked at himself in the mirror, like he did every day, before he went back up to the noisy world.

It was the same boy looking back at him: quiet, shy Alex. The loneliest boy in the world. Not exactly bullied or anything, because the school took a very stern stand on bullying and didn't allow it. No, not bullied. But not popular, not well-liked. Pretty much friendless, if you wanted to know the truth. Well, except for his cat.

He was the boy who didn't want anyone to see him. Not really.

"I almost wish I was someone else sometimes," he said to his reflection.

He picked up his bag and walked out. Maybe just a little faster than usual. He did a quick peek over his shoulder before the door closed behind him. He wasn't *scared* or anything, but he could have sworn that after he spoke, his reflection in the mirror …

… winked.

Just once.

And he knew he hadn't winked at himself.
Because it wasn't like him to wink.
It wasn't like Alex at all.

CHAPTER 2

ALEX THE INVISIBLE

In Alex's first class after lunch, he tried not to think about the wink.

His teacher called his name twice before she noticed him. He had to raise his voice to make himself heard, which wasn't that unusual.

"Oh! There you are, Alex! Next time, speak up!" Then she went on to the next name.

In gym, his class played basketball. And just like every week, his gym teacher, Mr. Timbert, put him on a team last.

"Oh, Alex! Right, I forgot about you. You can join the blue team," he said absently, not even looking up. He handed Alex the rejected blue bib, rejected because it was torn and faded, which Alex pulled over his head without complaint. Alex didn't think it was on purpose — Mr. Timbert was nice enough — it was just that, like everyone else, he hardly noticed Alex. Ever. Which wasn't fair, since Alex was great at basketball. He called to get the ball, which only came to him if someone missed a pass. Which was almost never.

The truth was, he sank baskets whenever he actually got the ball. But no one noticed when he did, or they thought someone else had done it. He didn't stop trying, though. Because one of the few things he knew for sure? He was good at basketball.

During library time, the librarian forgot once again to order the book he'd been waiting for: *The World Book of Cats.*

"I'm so sorry, Alex! I keep forgetting. I'll order it for you now, okay?" Alex nodded. But he knew she'd forget. Again.

In science class, his bean plant wasn't doing too well. Everyone else had a bean plant that was green and leafy and climbing toward the light, straining to live. But even though it was planted at the same time, his was just starting out. Struggling even. Two little leaves trembled on a sickly, skinny stalk. Mr. Timbert (who also taught him science) said, "Don't worry, Allan, some beans take longer than others to get started."

"Thanks, Mr. Timbert," Alex said. He didn't correct his teacher. After two years in his class, Mr. Timbert sometimes still got his name wrong and called him "Allan." Alex wasn't even sure if Mr. Timbert realized he also taught him gym.

The last class of the day was music. Alex played the only instrument that no one else wanted: the percussion section. Which sounds like it might be drums, but in fact wasn't. Alex played everything *but* drums, which were played by a boy that everyone knew and liked.

Alex stood beside this popular boy whose name was Bertram, Ram for short (which was a good name), and played the triangle, or the maracas, or the xylophone, none of which was even a tiny bit interesting.

And no one noticed. Because they never did.

And Alex didn't complain, or make a fuss, or draw any attention to himself.

Because he never did, either.

CHAPTER 3

THE CLEARING

That evening after dinner, Alex stomped through the snow to the barn. He patted the horses, Minnie and his own horse, Pins. He slipped Pins an apple, which she ate with big chomps. The barn was peaceful, warm, and Alex liked the smell of hay and horses.

His best friend, Needles, sat cleaning her fur on a straw bale.

Needles was a Norwegian Forest Cat. She was big and silver-haired, with enormous yellow eyes. She didn't mind winter or snow at all. Her tufted paws kept her on top of the snow, and her thick fur kept her warm and dry.

Needles was better than a dog. Because she was a cat.

She could climb trees, for one thing. What dog could do that?

The barn was really the only place that Alex felt happy. Or safe. With his two best friends, Needles and Pins.

He said good night to the horses, then slipped out of the barn. He looked over at the house. Carl sat in the living room in front of the computer. Alex could see him through the big kitchen window. Then Alex looked over at the dark woods.

Technically, he wasn't supposed to go into the woods at night.

Technically.

There was an old wives' tale about the place. About strange lights and voices and more nonsense, which Alex didn't believe and had never seen.

Still, his parents had told him not to go in there after dark.

But his parents weren't around, were they? If they didn't want him to go in there, maybe they shouldn't leave him alone all the time. Maybe they should rethink going halfway around the world for research. And Carl, the person who was *supposed* to be looking after him, wouldn't even notice.

"Mrowl?"

"Yes, yes, let's go," Alex whispered.

Alex and Needles slipped across the yard and into the dark woods. Needles ran on top of the deep snow on wide, soft paws.

Alex stomped along the path. The trees blotted out the sky as the pair disappeared into the forest. But it didn't matter, Needles could see in the dark perfectly, being a cat, and Alex knew where he was going, too. They walked the woods together all the time. The friends slipped along the winding pathway, farther into the gloom …

… and there it was.

The moonlit clearing. The dark trees stood, tall and a little spooky, all around the edge. At the centre of the clearing was a soft billow of snow.

At the far side stood a tiny abandoned cabin. The cabin was over one hundred years old, built back when trappers camped in the woods. It had an old, patched roof, a covered porch, and a creaky door, but no one ever came here. It was a perfect spot to be alone.

It was Alex's secret place.

Alex watched the moonlight glow behind the trees. Then, as if on cue, a gentle snowfall started.

"Needles! It's snowing!" Needles jumped and batted at snowflakes. They tried to catch snowflakes together at the edge of the woods.

Alex was about to step farther out of the trees …

… but stopped.

For the first time ever, there was something else in the clearing.

How did I not notice that?

He stared. Needles stared, too.

A pile of … something … lay in the snow. It wasn't a big pile; if anything it looked like a bicycle in a heap. Which was maybe why Alex hadn't seen it at first.

But it was there.

And gently on fire.

It was glowing softly green, too.

Alex gulped.

"Meow?"

"Yes, I know, Needles. I see it," Alex whispered.

Needles turned her yellow eyes on Alex and jumped onto the cabin porch. She began to carefully lick ice from her paws.

"What is it?" Alex asked his cat. She stopped licking her paws and watched him.

"I'm going to look," Alex whispered. He crept into the clearing, closer and closer to the wisps of smoke — or was it steam? — rising slowly into the snowy moonlight.

A few more steps, and Alex stood over the pile. It didn't make sense. A ball of metal, twisted and melted onto itself, lay in a clearing. The ground was scorched, the winter grass blackened, the snow melted away. A few puffs of smoke rose off the metal, so it hadn't been there long. And it wasn't very big. Not even as big as a bike, now that he was closer to it.

The strangest thing, though, was the glowing ooze. Little green puddles gathered at the edge of the pile.

"Maybe it's toxic?" Alex backed away, keeping his boots clear. He didn't know what he was looking at, but glowing green ooze probably wasn't good.

"MREOWWL!" Alex looked up at his cat ...

... and froze.

A tall figure stood at the edge of the forest.

No, there were TWO tall figures. Perfectly still. Watching him.

He slowly took a step backward.

"Are you The Other?" a strange, raspy voice called out.

"W-w-what?"

"Are you The Other?" the weird voice came again.

"N-n-o! I don't think so?" Alex was too scared to run. The figures were tall, too tall, halfway-up-the-trees tall. They hid just behind the last tree, hard to see. A weird little breeze sprang up, and the trees around the cabin started to sway.

A foggy green light rose around them with the breeze.

"Have you seen The Other?" The voice wasn't like anything he'd ever heard before, partway between a rasp and a squeal. The figures didn't move.

"No?" Alex's throat was dry. He took another step backward in the snow, back toward the path. Needles ran to his side, her hair on end.

Which made her look enormous. And scared.

"Beware The Other," the eerie voice rasped. Alex gulped.

"Oh. Okay!" He took another step backward. He did NOT want to turn his back on the dark strangers. The weird voices.

"Thank you!" he called, edging closer to the path. One more step back. One of the figures moved into the clearing. Then the second one. The moonlight shone on them, the snow fell around them, but Alex couldn't quite make out what they were.

Tall strangers. Too tall. In a strange green fog in the dark.

They took a step toward him, in perfect unison.

They had bright green eyes!

Alex stared. Then he turned and fled.

"NEEDLES! RUN!" Alex tore back down the path. Blindly. He fell and tripped in the snow, banged a knee, lost a mitten. Needles ran beside him.

Soon Alex could see the horse barn beside the house. He jumped over the paddock fence, then stopped, gasping for air. The kitchen light was on. Something about the kitchen light being on made him feel slightly better.

Kitchens were normal, where people did normal things.

The weird breeze stopped as suddenly as it had started. Alex stood gasping in the moonlight, all ears and eyes. Listening. Watching. But the woods were still.

Something moved in the tree above him. Alex looked up into the wide eyes of his cat.

There was a tiny blob of green on her tail. The ooze from the clearing!

"Needles! Come down!" Alex called. Needles stared at him from the tree, twitching her tail with the green blob.

Then she hissed, *"Beware THE OTHER!"*

Alex let out a screech that made birds fly out of the tree. One of the horses in the barn answered with a frightened neigh. Alex tore across the yard, through the kitchen door, and up to his room.

Carl was on the computer as Alex ran by. He didn't notice his little brother.

But then Carl hardly noticed anything when it came to Alex.

CHAPTER 4

FUSS ON THE BUS

Alex lay in bed with the covers pulled up to his chin.

He tossed, he turned, he stared out the window at the stormy sky, the pitch-black forest.

He shivered and worried all night long.

What was going on?

Beware The Other....

There was NO WAY his cat *said* that. He must have had a reaction to the tall strangers in the forest. The green stuff, the pile of smoking junk in the clearing. It was all weird.

Maybe I'm coming down with something? Alex thought.

The problem was, he wasn't sick. In fact, he felt fine. It occurred to him that maybe, just maybe, he should tell someone. But really, other than his parents, who would he tell? And *they* just happened to be on the other side of the planet, anyway.

And Carl was right out.

He'd never told Carl anything in his life, and he wasn't about to start now. And anything he did say would just sound crazy.

My reflection winked at me this morning in the mirror at school.

Then tonight, two tall ... whatever those were ... in the forest asked me about something called The Other. And there was this strange green goo in the snow.

Oh, and Needles talked to me, too. Like, with words.

When dawn came, he decided that he must have imagined the whole thing. He didn't like to admit it, but he always got a little jumpy when his parents went away. Especially at first. He quietly got out of bed, dressed, and tip-toed past Carl snoring in the guest room.

Even his snoring sounded like a whistle.

Alex slipped out the kitchen door and into the dark, cold morning. Needles wasn't in the tree. She wasn't in the barn with Pins and Minnie. She wasn't at the back door asking for her breakfast.

Where *was* she?

Alex looked for his cat for over an hour. At seven o'clock, he heard Carl's pickup truck pull out of the laneway. But he kept looking. It wasn't that unusual for Needles to stay out overnight, even in the middle of the winter. She hardly ever slept in the house, anyway, preferring the barn. It wasn't even that unusual for her to disappear for a few days now and then.

But she'd never *talked* before. That was definitely on the unusual side.

Alex bit his lip raw worrying about where she might be. But he had to give up look- ing. The school bus would be there soon. He went into the kitchen and made a quick breakfast of oatmeal and orange juice. There was a handwritten note on the table: *Gone to McGregor's farm. Some trouble with panicky pigs. Carl.*

When Alex's watch said 7:35 a.m., he had to go. He grabbed an apple and went out into the cold morning. He called for Needles a few more times, but she wasn't anywhere.

He took a few bites from his apple. He rounded the barn.

And stopped.

A girl stood at the end of the lane. She had her back to him.

This had never happened before. Alex's farm was in the middle of nowhere, outside of town. There were no kids around, no farms nearby. The nearest farm was the McGregor's, way down the road. And they didn't have any girls. Old Farmer McGregor lived alone.

Alex gulped and drew up his courage. He crunched as quietly as he could down the snowy lane.

"Hello, Alex," the girl said without turning around. She kept her back to him. She had a long, thick braid down her back.

He stopped. "Um, hello? Do I know you?" Now he was closer, he saw that she was wearing jeans, a blue shirt, a ski jacket, winter boots, and gloves, exactly like his. She was his height. His size. Her hair was the same colour and just like his, except for her braid. He didn't have one of those.

There was something odd about it, though.

Then, very slowly her braid … moved. It

twitched, then began a slow wag, from side to side.

His heart started to pound.

"W-w-who are you?"

"I think you know who I am, Alex," the girl whispered.

Then she turned around. A face like no other stared at him. A face that looked almost exactly like his if he were a girl.

And a *cat*.

Alex tried to scream, but nothing came out. He went weak in the knees. He dropped his apple … and stared.

The girl's face was covered in fur; even her ears were furry. She opened her mouth and smiled, a startling, pointy-toothed smile. Her long braid swayed gently back and forth.

Just like a cat's tail!

The girl bent and picked up Alex's half-eaten apple.

She took a bite.

Alex was just about to yell at her to get away from him when the school bus drove into view. He ran to the end of the lane and threw up his arms.

"Help me! HELP!" he shrieked. The bus stopped in the snowy road, and the door opened. Alex leapt on and shouted, "There's a weird cat girl out there! Help!"

"Sit down, kid," the bus driver snarled and pulled the door shut. Alex wheeled around, grabbed the back of the driver's seat, and looked at the laneway.

It was empty.

The girl was gone. Alex stared in disbelief as the bus drove away. He staggered to his seat and sat down as the bus lurched toward town.

"Oooh, a weird cat girl is after me," one kid mocked. Everyone laughed.

Alex didn't even care. He stared out the bus window with a horrible thought in his head: *That girl! That girl WAS A CAT!*

CHAPTER 5

THE REFLECTION

Alex sat on the bus, trying hard not to panic.

The weird strangers in the clearing last night, Needles ... now that *girl*.

I wonder what it feels like to go crazy? Would I know I'm going crazy, if I was? he wondered. He stared out the window. Someone whipped a rotten sandwich past him, but he didn't even flinch. He hardly noticed. It wasn't meant for him, anyway. Probably.

When he got to school, he walked the halls in a daze. He sat in math class, barely listening. He was good at math. Whenever he knew the answer to a question, he usually put up his hand.

But today he didn't.

Alex sat through art class and made a passable drawing of a bowl of fruit. The art teacher hardly noticed, but Alex was too preoccupied to care.

Something very, very strange was going on. Possibly he wasn't quite as totally *sane* as he should be.

Who *was* that girl? Or *what*?

He slowly decided that whoever she was, he must have been so worried about his cat he imagined that she looked like one.

It must have been a hallucination.

Whatever was happening, he needed to be alone. To think.

At lunchtime, Alex planned to vanish quietly into the basement. He didn't really want to go back down there, not after the wink yesterday, but it was the only place he could be alone.

Besides, much weirder things are going on here than a wink, anyway. Maybe I DID wink at myself yesterday.

He slipped past all the kids laughing and pushing each other as they lined up for the lunchroom. He slid along the hallway, and no one noticed. He walked silently past the boiler room in the basement and opened the creaky, technically off-limits boy's bathroom door.

The bathroom was empty.

As usual.

Alex settled against the wall, but he was too upset to eat. There was nothing at all normal about whatever was happening. He looked down at his hands. They trembled a little.

He stood up and held on to the sink. He looked into the mirror ...

... it was just him in there.

His quiet, shy face.

"What's going on? Am I going crazy?" he asked his reflection.

"Don't ask me," his reflection answered.

Alex jumped back. He stared, his mouth open....

"Wh-what?" he whispered.

"I said, 'Don't ask me,'" his reflection repeated. "I'm in here, you're out there. I'm pretty sure you know as much about our state of mind as I do."

His reflection took a step back, deeper into the mirror, and crossed his arms. Except for the different movements, it was Alex's reflection in there. Same clothes. Same hair. Even the same tiny fleck of mud from the barn on his sleeve.

Same Alex. But *not*.

"Don't look so surprised. You saw me yesterday, remember?" his reflection said. Then his reflection winked. Alex-outside-the-mirror shook his head, opened and closed his eyes. Just then a snowball hit the outside of the bathroom window, hard, and Alex-outside-the-mirror jumped. His reflection didn't.

"I don't believe you're really talking to me," Alex whispered and closed his eyes. But when he opened them again, there he was. His reflection, with his arms crossed, shaking his head.

"Why wouldn't I be talking to you?" Alex's reflection said. "You can be you in lots of different ways at the same time, you know. And frankly, you need a friend right now. I mean, does anyone even KNOW you're down here? Do you even HAVE any friends?"

Alex put his hands on the sink and drew up close to the mirror. He looked at himself, made a face, stuck his tongue out. His reflection just smiled at him.

"Cute," his reflection said.

"But … how is this happening?" Alex-outside-the-mirror whispered. Alex and his reflection were nose-to-nose, which is pretty much what you expect when you look at yourself in a mirror. Except his reflection wasn't him. Or was, but it wasn't doing any of the things he was doing.

"Look, Alex," his reflection said gently. "You're under stress. You've seen some strange things in the past twenty-four hours. I don't blame you if you think you're cracking up. But I'm here to tell you something important." Alex's reflection looked genuinely concerned.

"You have to watch out for that girl with the braid, Alex," his reflection whispered.

"How do you know about her?"

His reflection rolled his eyes just a little.

"I AM you, you know. I do KNOW things. Now listen. This is important. You have to beware ..."

Don't say The Other....

"... The Other."

Alex gripped the sink so tightly, his hands hurt. "I know that. Those tall strangers told me last night. Even my cat told me that! But what IS The Other, anyway?"

He swayed slightly, leaned into the sink, and stared at himself.

"I don't know! How would I know?" his reflection answered. "I'm in here, remember?

That's what YOU have to find out! Do a little investigating, why don't you? You could start by trying to get people to notice you, be less invisible to everyone," Alex-inside-the-mirror said. "You're practically fading away, my friend," his reflection added.

Alex was about to answer, but the bathroom door opened.

Which had never happened before.

The janitor stuck his head in the room and was startled to see Alex standing there, clutching the sink in front of the mirror.

"Hey, kid, you okay? I heard voices." Alex just stared at the man. He was so out of place, so unexpected, that for a second Alex wasn't sure he was real.

"Shouldn't you be out throwing snowballs with your friends?" the janitor said, not totally unkindly. "Scram," he added nicely. This was a new janitor, much younger than the usual janitor.

"Are you new or something?" Alex asked, gathering his lunch together and stuffing everything into his backpack.

The janitor shook his head. "Nope, not really. Not unless six months of working here is new. You've just never noticed me before. Now out," he said, shuffling Alex out the door.

Alex took one last look at the mirror before the man hustled him out into the hallway. There was no one in the mirror. Nothing winked back at him. The mirror was empty.

Which is pretty much what you expect from mirrors, when there is nothing to reflect.

CHAPTER 6

NOW YOU SEE ME …

Alex left the bathroom. The janitor said goodbye with a cheerful wave and went back to mopping the floor.

Alex walked up the stairs to the sound of kids getting ready for an afternoon of school. The bell rang, and he barely heard it. He walked in a fog, his face set, his eyebrows drawn together.

He was trying very hard to tell himself that whatever just happened in the bathroom mirror wasn't real. He had to have imagined it. That, along with everything else weird since last night.

What's happening to me?

Alex looked down at his hands. His feet. He was really there.

But he didn't feel like he was. He was beginning to feel very strangely NOT there. Like he was split in two. All over the place. The bell rang again, and it was time for his first afternoon class. A group of bigger kids headed toward him, laughing and talking.

You could start by trying to get people to notice you, be less invisible to everyone....

Alex stepped into the middle of the hall.

The loud, laughing kids moved around him, like water around a rock in a stream. They jostled him. But they didn't look at him.

They didn't see me!

Alex ran down the hall and burst into his classroom. He ran to his chair, pulled out his books, and no one noticed him. The teacher took attendance and checked off his name without looking up.

Alex did his work quietly. He went to French class. He sat and conjugated verbs, he repeated French sentences back to the teacher, just like it was a normal day.

But nothing was normal. HE wasn't normal.

He got through the day. Somehow. He tried to put his hand up as often as he could.

He tried to make people notice him, but he'd spent so long being invisible, everyone was used to him not really being there.

Even his reflection in the haunted bathroom mirror knew that.

Alex tried not to think about his reflection.

At the end of the day, he stood in line for the school bus. The line moved forward. Just as Alex was about to get on, the driver shut the door in his face and drove away.

The bus driver didn't see me!

Alex gulped. THAT had never happened before!

He pulled out his cellphone to call his brother for a ride home, but it was dead. Of course. He didn't have any friends to call; the only person he ever texted was his mother, so he hardly ever used it. Not enough to remind himself to plug it in regularly, anyway.

Alex zipped up his winter coat and tugged his wool hat onto his head. He started the long, cold walk home.

CHAPTER 7

PANICKY PIGS

The winter sunlight cut across the dark trees, and a cool breeze blew over the fields. The snow clung to Alex's boots, slowly soaking through to his socks.

He walked home in the darkening afternoon. An hour later, frozen and snow-covered, he walked up the laneway to his house. He slipped into the barn.

Maybe Needles will be in here….

"Needles! Where are you?" But his beautiful cat didn't appear. The horses looked up, though, at the sound of his voice, then went back to their fresh hay.

He sat in the straw and tried to warm up. A tear started at the corner of his eye, and he angrily brushed it away. He missed his cat, wherever she was. If she was there, he'd feel so much better.

What am I going to do? I'm going crazy. I should probably tell someone about the strangers, the girl…. I could leave out my reflection talking to me maybe, for now. And poor Needles. I hope she's okay. But even if I was going to ask for help, who would I tell? And what would I say?

He listened to the horses eating. It calmed him. Whatever was going on, at least the barn was the same place, even if his cat wasn't in it. Soon it was dark out, and he was getting hungry. He said good night to the horses and walked to the house. He looked over at the forest and called his cat a few times. But she wasn't out there.

He walked in the back door. Into the kitchen. And stopped.

"Yes, green fog. You heard me. And panicked pigs." Carl was talking to their parents through the computer.

He heard his mother say, "Green *fog*?" His father said, "Panicked *pigs*?"

Green fog? Alex listened more closely.

"That's not all," Carl said quietly. "Old McGregor also says that two of his piglets vanished!"

"What about a green fog?" Alex stepped into the living room.

Carl turned around, surprised. "Alex! You're late! Snowball fight with friends after school or something? Here, talk to Mom and Dad while I get you some dinner."

"No really, what about the green fog?" Alex demanded. He was too tired and cold to tell Carl about missing the bus. Or no. He didn't miss it. IT missed *him*.

"Oh, it's nothing, just old Farmer McGregor. You know him and his weird stories. A giant's hand, now vanishing pigs — the old man is kind of crazy." Carl rolled his eyes, then stirred some delicious-smelling soup on the stove.

Alex sat in front of the computer screen. His parents looked out at him. It was sunny and warm where they were. They were wearing short-sleeved shirts. His mom looked like she was already a little tanned.

"Alex, are you … are you okay?" she asked. He felt his bottom lip tremble. He dropped his head and looked at his hands.

"Yes," he said.

"Are you sure, Alex? You look a little pale," his mother said. The sound of her voice made him sad. He pushed away the feeling that he really, really wanted her to hug him. She couldn't. Being half a world away.

"Actually, I was going to say he looked a little green around the gills," his father added. *Hilarious, Dad.*

"I'm fine," Alex lied.

"Well, what have you been doing this week?" His mother could tell there was something wrong. But what, really, could he possibly say?

My cat is missing, there's a terrifying girl out there, my reflection is talking to me, not to mention weirdly tall strangers. And The Other. Whatever that is, I'm supposed to beware it. You already know about the green fog. Come to think of it, quite a bit, Mom.

"Not much."

"Are you sure you're okay? You really do look awfully pale," his mother pressed.

"We can almost see through you, son!" his father joked.

Not funny, Dad. His parents talked for a while about whatever they were studying in the soil in Australia. They were botanists. And Alex couldn't even grow a healthy bean plant.

He didn't say much more, but he did nod a little when his mother said, "You know we miss you, right, Alex?"

He said goodnight, signed off the computer, and sat at the kitchen table to eat Carl's soup.

There was a piece of paper beside Carl's empty bowl.

Alex could just make out the word "fog" on the paper. He eyed Carl, who had his back to him. He was at the computer, playing online chess.

Alex made a noise with his soup spoon and quietly turned the paper toward him. It was a photocopy of an old newspaper clipping. Alex could see a part of the headline, "Frequent Fog Patches ..." His heart beat just a little faster. Carefully, Alex pulled the paper toward him, bit by bit.

Carl cleared his throat, but he didn't turn around.

The headline read, "Frequent Fog Patches Cause Panic Among Local Pigs." The date on the photocopy said "1907."

Over one hundred years ago!

Alex read quickly. The first line of the news story said, "Mr. Ebner Fingles put his farm up for sale after 104 years in the family. 'No comment,' Mr. Fingles said when asked to discuss his panicky pigs. His wife, however, said, 'Them pigs was acting very strange the other night, after that green fog rolled over the barnyard. That's not the worst part, though, those two tall strangers, with their awful weird voices …'"

Carl walked into the room, grabbed the paper from Alex, and stuffed it into his coat pocket. He frowned down at Alex, who tried to look innocent. Carl was no good with children, not even his little brother.

"Mrs. Cody, the town librarian, gave this to old Farmer McGregor. It might explain about the pigs," Carl finally said. "But I think it's nonsense." Alex stared up at his brother.

"What's nonsense? All it says is that green fog made the pigs scared, and something about strangers," Alex said innocently.

"Forget about it, it's silly. I'm going to town for a few hours," Carl said, likely because he couldn't think of anything else to say. Then he whistled out the back door, and Alex heard his brother's pickup truck drive away.

Alex spent the rest of the night on his bed in the dark, staring at the ceiling.

Green fog? Tall strangers? Awful voices?

He fell asleep thinking his town was weird, and a little scary. He tried very hard NOT to think about a pile of green goo in the snow or the two weird voices in the darkness.

Or Needles.

Or The Other, whatever that was.

He tossed and turned all night. If he'd looked outside, though, he would have seen two tall, dark figures at the edge of the forest, looking up at his window.

An eerie green fog rolled around them as they watched. And waited.

CHAPTER 8

BOY WHO IS
KNOWN AS ALEX

The alarm buzzed: 7:06 a.m. Alex had to hurry to catch the school bus!

When did I fall asleep? He dressed in the dark, headed down to the kitchen. His brother had left him a message on the table: *Gone to McGregor's to help with pigs again. Cereal for breakfast.*

Alex ate, packed a fast lunch, grabbed his boots and coat, and ran outside. It was 7:36. He was going to miss the bus! It was a cold morning, but bright. The trees waved and moaned in the forest, an eerie sound. A brisk wind swept over the frozen fields.

He ran past the barn — he wanted to see if Needles was in there, but there was no time — and turned to jog down the lane. The bus was already there! For the first time ever, it was early. The school bus door was wide open, and someone got on!

Someone with a *long braid*.

"WAIT! Stop!" Alex ran as fast as he could toward the bus, but the driver shut the door. Alex stopped and stared, his warm breath puffing into the frozen air.

The girl with the braid pushed her way down the school bus aisle. She dropped into a seat and looked out the window.

She waved at him and smiled. A nasty smile, too.

She didn't look like a cat, anymore, which was a definite relief. But she looked weirdly familiar. Like him. A *lot* like him, if he were a girl, maybe.

The bus lurched into gear and roared off down the road. Alex watched it disappear.

Who is she? And what am I going to do now?

With a moan, he realized his phone was still dead and in the house on the kitchen table. He could call Carl for a ride, but Carl was working on McGregor's farm. Besides, he was as bad at charging his phone as Alex.

Alex looked around the deserted, snowy road. His mountain bike in the tool shed! It would be a cold ride to school, but he could do it. He'd done it before, and at least he wouldn't have to walk all the way. He thought about the horses and the sleigh under a tarp in the barn. Not so many years ago he could have hitched Pins up to the sleigh to get to school.

But no one did that anymore.

He took a few steps toward the tool shed.

And stopped.

Someone was watching him. He could feel their eyes on him. He tried not to turn around, but they were there. At the corner of his eye.

Not one, but *two* someones. Two tall, dark figures stood across the road. They stood behind the trees, almost out of sight. They wore long overcoats and dark sunglasses. An eerie breeze picked up and danced snow across the trees.

Alex's heart beat hard as he walked, just a little faster, toward the shed. A strange, squealing voice cut across the wind.

"Boy Who Is Known as Alex." The voice made the hair on his neck stand up.

"Have you seen The Other?" a second voice said.

Alex kept walking, keeping one eye on them, one eye on the shed door. Three more steps … slowly … slowly …

Two nights ago in the clearing, he hadn't seen them that well.

This was daytime. He could see them perfectly. They were tall. Too tall. They stood in the ditch, and they were still way above Alex's head. And oddly skinny. Their overcoats looked wrong on their tall, slender bodies. They went right down to the ground, so you couldn't see their feet. They'd jammed their hands into their pockets.

Alex got the feeling they were hiding them.

He slowly edged toward the shed, toward his bike. He turned his head.

"What do you want?" he called, closer to his bike.

"We seek The Other," the first stranger said. Alex noticed they didn't have steamy breath rising from them when they spoke, like he did. He gulped.

"Beware The Other," the second one added. The first stranger took a step out of the ditch and towered above him across the snowy

road. A strange foot (if it WAS a foot) peeked out from beneath the long coat. It clattered on the ice.

Clip. Clop.

Alex bolted into the shed. He jumped on his bike and pedalled across the snowy driveway in a blur.

He looked back over his shoulder once, when he made it to the road.

What are they?

The two figures stood and watched him ride away, their heads slightly tilted. They looked like curious dogs.

One of them squealed, *"We can help you, Boy Who Is Known as Alex."* And now Alex knew exactly what the strange voice sounded like: a squealing *pig*!

If a pig ever took it into its head to talk....

He pedalled faster, but not fast enough. Above the roaring in his ears, he heard the second grunting, piggy voice squeal, *"Boy Who Is Known as Alex, let us help you."*

Alex put his head down and charged along the highway toward school.

CHAPTER 9

THE GIRL WITH
THE BRAID

Alex rode faster than he thought he could. *That's it! I'm definitely cracking up! Everything is WAY TOO weird! I need to tell someone what's happening to me! I'm going to get Carl to make me an appointment with Dr. Philips this afternoon!*

He pulled his scarf over his nose, and it froze to his face. But he didn't care. He barely felt the cold.

He arrived at school half an hour late. He ran to his locker, changed into his shoes, and hung up his coat. He snuck past the principal's office, and no one noticed. No teachers stopped him.

The school was silent, and Alex slipped along the halls in a daze.

He crept into the classroom behind the teacher, and she didn't tell him to get a late slip. He walked down the aisle to his desk, and no one looked up.

When he got to his seat, *someone* was already sitting there.

The girl with the braid looked at him. Her pencil was poised over his math book.

"Hi, Alex," she said quietly. Alex stared at the girl.

"What are you doing here? In my desk? Writing in *my* math book?"

"Shhh," the girl whispered, because the teacher was looking over at them. Alex stared at the girl. She wasn't covered in fur like the day before. Her long braid didn't sway back and forth, either. She was just a girl.

A girl who, except for the braid, looked *exactly* like him.

He looked at her for another moment, then pulled a chair from the back of the classroom. He sat at the desk with her. *His* desk.

"Who are you, anyway? And why have you been waiting for the school bus at *my* stop?" he whispered. He made a grab for the math book, and she pulled it away.

"Is it your stop, though?" She stared at him innocently ...

... then for a second her eyes shone *bright green*!

Glowing-goo green.

Alex's eyes grew wide.

"WHO ARE YOU?!" he shrieked, jumping up. His chair fell over.

The teacher came down the aisle.

"Is everything okay?" she asked. Alex was about to answer that this strange girl was sitting in *his* desk, obviously, but the girl answered first.

"I'm sorry, I just dropped my pencil," she said politely.

The teacher smiled at the girl with the braid. "Okay, well try to drop your pencil more quietly next time, please, Alex," she said and went back to the front of the class.

Alex felt a scream start deep in his chest.

The teacher said to please be quiet. But she didn't ask *them* to be quiet.

She asked the *girl with the braid* to be quiet. And when the teacher said, "Alex," she wasn't looking at him. The teacher was look-ing at *her*.

But worse, far worse than all that, for a second, the teacher's eyes had turned BRIGHT GREEN.

Alex backed away from the girl with the braid.

"Wh-at … what's happening?"

"Isn't it obvious, Alex?" the girl answered. Very slowly, the girl's braid began to sway, back and forth, back and forth. Alex stared, his mouth open in horror.

The girl went on. "You're basically invisible to most people in this town, aren't you, Alex? You're the perfect choice. You're making this much too easy. Even your cat fought harder than you. I still can't quite get rid of her tail.…"

The girl's braid swayed gently from side to side.

"My … my *cat*? Her *tail*? What do you mean? What have you done to Needles?" His voice was a hoarse, terrified whisper. A terrible thought was forming, but he didn't want to think it through to the end.

I still can't quite get rid of her tail.…

The girl drew close to him. She pinned Alex up against the wall next to the desk, almost touching him. The rest of the class had their heads down, working quietly. No one noticed.

"Don't worry, your cat will be fine. She makes a wonderful host."

"Host? Please ... please tell me what's going on," Alex begged. His heart pounded, his mouth was dry....

"You don't *seem* stupid, but I guess I have to spell it out for you," the girl hissed. She drew closer to him, nose-to-nose. The teacher, the students worked away, not noticing.

If I called for help, would they even hear me?

"Ever heard of an *evil twin*, Alex?" the girl whispered. "In German, they call it a *doppelgänger*."

"A ... a *what*?"

The girl narrowed her eyes. He had the oddest feeling that, just for a second, he was looking into his own eyes.

"'Beware The Other,' Alex. You've heard that lately, haven't you?"

Alex nodded.

"Yes, but ... what IS it?" His voice was so low, he wasn't sure she heard him. But she did. She grinned, a nasty grin.

"Don't I look *awfully* familiar, Alex? Don't you feel like you're *almost* looking at yourself when you look at me? Thanks for the apple yesterday, by the way. It's just what I needed."

"*Needed*?" Alex whispered. "What do you mean? *Needed*?"

At that second the bell rang. The class stood up. The girl turned away, and Alex reached out to stop her.

"OWWWW!" His hand! His hand *burned* where he touched her arm!

"Don't try to grab me again, or you'll be sorry," she warned. Alex clutched his scorched hand and stared at her.

"But who *are* you? Please ... please tell me!"

The girl pulled in close and whispered softly in his ear. "Don't you know by now, Alex? Why you should beware The Other?" Alex shook his head, and the girl grinned that nasty grin again.

"Because I'M The Other," she breathed.

"Think of me as *an 'other' you*. A *better* you. First I was your cat. But thanks to your apple, minute by minute, now I'm becoming *you*. Soon, I'll BE you. And you'll be gone. You're practically invisible already, though, aren't you, Alex?"

Then she tossed her head and turned away. The girl with the braid — The Other — left the classroom. She joined a group of kids and told a joke, and everyone laughed. No one seemed to realize they didn't know this new girl. No one even asked who she was.

As Alex watched in horror, clutching his burned hand, the girl and all his classmates turned to look at him.

And for a second ... *all of their eyes burned bright green.*

CHAPTER 10

THE OTHER

Alex shrieked. But no one heard him.

I've gone completely crazy!

He ran down the hallway behind his class and the girl with the braid.

The Other Alex.

"But you don't even know her!" he yelled at his classmates, but no one listened. The kids in his class crowded around The Other Alex. They treated her like they'd known her forever. They wanted to sit with her. They wanted to be science partners. They wanted her to go to sleepovers that weekend.

The real Alex stood at the door of the

science room, his heart beating fast.

"But you don't even know her," he called again, quieter. Still no one listened.

The Other Alex sat at *his* desk. She picked up *his* sickly bean plant. She started her assignment — *his* assignment. When Mr. Timbert took attendance and called his name, she answered, "Here."

The class settled down to work. No one looked at him standing there at the door, not even once. If he didn't feel invisible before, he did now. And he didn't just *feel* invisible. To his class and his teachers, he really *was*.

I have to make them see me!

"Mr. Timbert! Mr. Timbert! I'm right here!" Alex yelled. He banged a chair on the floor. He slammed the door as loudly as he could a few times. But the class went on quietly. No one even looked up.

Well, one person did. The Other Alex. She laughed, shook her head, and showed him what she had in her hands …

… a big, leafy, healthy bean plant. *His* bean plant!

How did she do that? My plant was dying!

The real Alex and The Other Alex looked at each other for a moment longer … then the real Alex turned and ran to the principal's office.

Okay! You win! I don't know what's going on, but I need help!

He burst into the office. "Can I use the phone to call my brother? I'm not feeling well," Alex said. The lady behind the office counter didn't look up. Alex raised his voice. "HELLO! I need to use the phone, please!" She still didn't look up.

Alex ran around the counter. He grabbed the office phone and dialed his home number. His brother answered.

"Hello?"

"Carl! It's Alex. I'm really not feeling well. I need you to come and get me!"

"Hello?" Carl said. "Is anyone there? Who is this?"

Alex looked at the phone in horror. Now his *brother* couldn't hear him?

"CARL! CARL, IT'S ME, ALEX!" Alex screamed into the phone.

"Alex? I can barely hear you, speak up," he said. Alex almost cried with relief. Finally, someone could hear him.

"Carl, I need you to pick me up, I'm not feeling well! I need to see Dr. Philips." Alex could hear his brother moving the phone around his ear.

"Okay, no problem. I'll be there in half an hour," Carl said. "Meet me out front."

Alex hung up. The woman behind the counter still hadn't looked up. Alex stared at her for a minute. The relief of hearing Carl's voice, of being heard by Carl, made him a little braver.

"Hey! Can you really not see me?" he shouted. She didn't look up. He waved his hands in front of her face a few times. Nothing.

But I'm not invisible! I'm right here!

He turned and ran back to his locker. Halfway there, the bell rang, and the hallway filled with students.

He stood in the middle of a flow of kids. He was the rock in the stream, the salmon swimming upriver, the one person going the wrong way. Everyone washed around him, barely bumping into him, but not seeing him, either.

Like he really, really wasn't there.

He fought his way to his locker. He tugged it open and stared. There were two identical sets of everything: two backpacks, two coats, two pairs of boots.

Where did that come from?

He shook his head, opened and closed his eyes. He reached in and grabbed a backpack, coat, and boots.

"Seeing double?" a voice breathed in his ear. Alex whipped around.

A boy stood there. Alex stared at his exact twin: a boy with *his* face, *his* hair, *his* body.

"I'm not the girl with the braid anymore, am I?" the boy whispered.

Alex shook his head in disbelief. "Who … who are you?" he croaked.

"First I was your cat, then the girl with the braid, now you. It happened faster than even I was expecting," the boy said. "Like I said, you made it too easy." Alex stared at the boy, his exact twin, in horror.

"But … but … you look just like me!" Alex whispered.

"You still don't get it, do you? I AM you now, Alex," the boy said. "I'm The Other. YOUR Other. And there can be only one of us."

Then The Other Alex laughed — *his* laugh — and stared back at the real Alex … with *bright green eyes.*

CHAPTER 11

THIS WON'T HURT A BIT

Alex ran down the hall, trailing his backpack and his coat. His vision blurred, his heart raced.

The Other! There's another me! That girl with the braid! She turned into me! Either that or … I'm going crazy!

He burst out of the school into the bright sunshine. Carl's pickup truck idled outside the school. Carl waved at him. Alex could have cried with relief.

He grabbed his bike and tossed it into the back, then jumped in. Carl looked over at Alex.

"What the heck's wrong with you? You look terrible!" Carl said. Alex tried to calm his breathing, his racing heart. His brother could see him and knew who he was. It was the first time all day someone had looked at him and seen him.

Other than those two tall strangers this morning.

"Carl, you can see me, right?" Alex asked. He closed his eyes. His voice was a hoarse whisper.

Carl nodded slowly. "Of course, Alex. You're sitting right there. Do you have a fever or something?"

"I … I don't know. I hope so." Alex looked at his brother. He wanted to tell him he thought he was losing his mind. But he couldn't say it. He just couldn't. He just didn't know his brother well enough. Didn't trust him enough. At the moment, Alex didn't even trust himself enough to say what was happening to him.

"Just take me to the doctor," Alex answered. "And thanks for coming."

"No problem," Carl said. "Oh, and after the doctor, I should drop you at Finkman's, right?"

Alex stared at his brother for a second. Finkman's? What was Finkman's? For a moment, he had no idea what his brother was talking about.

Then his mind clicked. Oh, yeah, it was Friday. The day he worked at Finkman's Pharmacy after school. He'd worked there for almost a year. He loved Mrs. Finkman. Stocking the pharmacy shelves every Friday was a highlight of his week.

How could he forget?

Alex nodded. "Yes, Finkman's. Thanks." It was so … Carl … to remember something as solidly real as Finkman's Pharmacy.

After that, Alex sat still and silent, staring out the window. Carl drove and whistled. But at that moment, Alex didn't even mind the whistling.

Carl could *see* him.

When they got to the doctor's office, Carl sat in the waiting room. Alex sat on the crinkly paper on the examining table, freezing in his socks and underwear. Dr. Philips listened to Alex's heart, looked into his ears, nose, throat.

"Well, Alex, I can't find anything wrong with you. You're as healthy as ever," Dr. Philips said kindly. He wore thick glasses and he stooped a little, but Dr. Philips had always been their family doctor. He knew Alex well.

"But is there something else bothering you, son?"

Alex bit his lip. How exactly do you tell a doctor that you think you're cracking up?

"Dr. Philips?"

"Yes, Alex?"

"Do people ever think that they might have an identical twin, when they don't?"

Dr. Philips looked at Alex with surprise. "Hmm, I think we all wonder if there's a duplicate of us out there somewhere. But unless you're really an identical twin, it's just a fantasy. Although recently a photographer took pictures of people from all over the world who looked a lot like each other. Maybe there are only so many faces out there." Dr. Philips smiled at Alex. "Does that help?" he asked.

Alex nodded. *No. Not really.*

"I was there when you were born, Alex. I promise you, you don't have a twin," Dr. Philips added. "You can get dressed now."

As Alex pulled on his clothes, Dr. Philips looked at Alex's chart, and frowned. "But, you know what? You really do need your booster shot." Alex watched the doctor's back as he shuffled around. He pulled out a needle …

… and Alex gasped. Doctor Philips quickly moved the needle behind his back. *But not before Alex saw what was in it!*

"Are you okay, Alex?" the doctor asked. He leaned in, concerned. "You look a little pale." Alex looked up into the doctor's face.

"Hold still now, young man, this won't hurt a bit."

"Doctor Philips?"

"Yes?"

"What's in that needle?"

The doctor grinned. "Oh, nothing serious. Just some measles, mumps, rubella vaccine and …" Just as Dr. Philips dipped forward, Alex leapt. He jumped under the doctor's arm and shot out the door. He ran down the hallway and out into the reception room.

Carl dropped his magazine and stared as his little brother sprinted past.

Alex burst out the heavy glass door and down the steps. He tore to the pickup truck and grabbed his bike. He ran with it, hopped on, and sped across the snowy parking lot as fast as he could. Carl and the astonished Dr. Philips stood at the door as he pedalled away.

They stared at Alex as he rode off.

Dr. Philips still held the needle. Carl's eyes, the doctor's eyes, the goo in the needle … everything *burned bright green!*

CHAPTER 12

FINKMAN'S PHARMACY

Alex rode to the edge of town. He had nowhere to go. Nowhere to hide.

The world's gone crazy! The teachers, the kids at school, now Carl and Dr. Philips. Not to mention me. Or The Other. What am I going to do?

He stared out at the windswept fields of snow. The highway ran south to the city from there.

Could I ride to the city? Live there? Do I know anyone there?

But it would never work. He was a twelve-year-old boy on a bike in the middle of nowhere. In the middle of winter. He had no money. No friends. He had a job, but how much did you need to live on, anyway? Probably more than he earned stocking the shelves at Finkman's for two hours a week.

But when he thought of Mrs. Finkman, he suddenly felt a tiny bit better.

Mrs. Finkman, the pharmacist, was the most normal, sensible person he knew. There was definitely no funny business about Finkman's Pharmacy or Mrs. Finkman.

If anyone could help him, it was her. She was his last hope. He rode his bike against the wind, across the icy road, and back into town. He hoped Carl wasn't looking for him, but he'd have to risk it. A few minutes later he pulled in front of the pharmacy.

"Mrs. Finkman!" The little bell over the door jangled as Alex ran in. It was so warm in the pharmacy, he suddenly realized how cold he was. He rubbed his hands together.

Please help me!

"Mrs. Finkman!" he called again. A pleasant-looking grey-haired lady stepped out from the stockroom at the back of the store.

Please see me, Mrs. Finkman!

He called her name again, and she looked up in surprise.

"Oh! Alex!" she said. "What are you doing here?" she asked, bewildered.

"It's Friday after school, Mrs. Finkman. When I come and sort the new stock?" How could she forget?

"Well, of course, dear, but it's just that you already did it." Mrs. Finkman looked puzzled.

"What do you mean, Mrs. Finkman? I just got here," Alex said.

Mrs. Finkman came from behind the pharmacist's counter, opened the little swing door to the stock floor, and peered into Alex's face.

"Are you okay, Alex? You look a little off," she said gently. She drew close to Alex, like she wanted to put her hand on his forehead and check for fever.

"Mrs. Finkman, I'm telling you, I just got here," he said. His mouth was dry, his heart started to pound. Mrs. Finkman was the nicest lady he knew. She was kind to him, paid him well, and always sent him home with a bag of peppermints each week. As the town's only pharmacist, she was everyone's friend. Finkman's Pharmacy donated new hockey jerseys for the town team every winter and new baseball team shirts every summer. Not that Alex had ever had either of those things. But still, everyone loved her.

She wouldn't tease him.

"Mrs. Finkman, I know this sounds crazy, but what do you mean that *I already stocked the shelves*?" Mrs. Finkman stared at him for a moment. Her grey hair was cut short, and her plastic tortoiseshell glasses almost hid her brown eyes.

"Well, you came in at lunchtime and told me you had to stock the shelves earlier than usual today, since you were busy tonight. I think you said you were going to a sleepover? And I said that was a first for you, and you seemed really happy...." She trailed off and looked at Alex.

He stared at her in horror.

"But I ... I didn't stock the shelves at lunch today, Mrs. Finkman. I promise you. I ... I was at the doctor." A horrible thought was forming in Alex's mind. If he didn't stock the shelves, who did?

Someone who *looked just like him*.

"Alex, are you feeling all right?" Mrs. Finkman drew in closer to Alex, reached for him, and he drew back in horror.

She cocked her head to one side and whispered, "Maybe you should get some *help*, Alex." Alex gulped and backed toward the door.

"I know two people who can help you. They're in the back. They were here asking about you, Alex. Let them help you." Mrs. Finkman reached out, but he dodged her and tore toward the door. He yanked the heavy door open, ran across the parking lot, and jumped on his bike.

He looked back over his shoulder once. Mrs. Finkman stood at her door. Two tall figures, much too tall, in overcoats and sunglasses, stood on either side of her. The three of them watched him ride away, like curious dogs.

Alex didn't feel the cold. He just rode and rode, anywhere.

As fast as he could.

CHAPTER 13

NO PLACE LIKE HOME

Alex rode along the highway.

He didn't want anyone to see him, and he didn't want to bump into Carl, those tall strangers, or anyone else with *green eyes*! If he was going to survive whatever was happening to him, he had to get home, fast. He needed supplies and somewhere to hide.

A storm was brewing. Dark clouds pulled across the sky, and snow started to fall. When he pulled into the driveway, the snow came hard and fast. He put his bike back in the shed.

He crept up the driveway. Carl's truck was parked outside the kitchen door. The horses stirred in the barn, but Alex didn't go to see them. He knew Needles wouldn't be in there, either.

The Other had done something with her. He couldn't bear to think what.

He hid behind the bushes at the side of the house. The driving snow hit his face.

He couldn't look away from the brightly lit kitchen.

And what he saw through the window.

Carl sat at the kitchen table. And so did a boy. The Other Alex.

The real Alex watched from outside in the snow as his evil twin sat across from Carl. The two looked warm and happy. They chatted and laughed together in the cozy kitchen.

The Other sat in *his* kitchen. In *his* house! Alex crept closer to the window and strained to hear what The Other Alex and Carl were saying.

But he could only catch a word or two.

"Needles."

"Doctor."

"Sorry. I feel better now."

Then, "tell Mom and Dad!" Carl jumped up. He called The Other Alex, and the two sat in front of the computer. Alex-outside-in-the-snow-and-storm couldn't hear anything. But he could see just fine. His mother's face came onto the computer screen. Then his father's face. They smiled, and then The Other Alex said something, and they all laughed.

Outside-Alex thought he heard the word "sleepovers" and "that's great, Alex!"

But it didn't matter if he heard a word. The happy look on his parents' faces told him that they thought they were talking to their son Alex. To *him*. A whole new Alex, maybe; a brand new boy who suddenly wasn't invisible and got invited to birthday parties and sleepovers.

They thought they were talking to a boy who was somehow taking a turn for the better.

Alex-outside-in-the-snow felt sick to his stomach. His teachers, his classmates, Mrs. Finkman, Carl. Now his mother and father.

The Other Alex had them all fooled.

Alex considered knocking on the kitchen door. But what if Carl didn't open it? Or even worse, what if he *did* but didn't see Alex? Then he'd be completely invisible. Gone. He didn't think he could handle that.

"But I'm right here," he whispered outside in the snow.

At least ... I think I am.

The real Alex was fading away. Unless he did something fast, the last piece of him, whoever he was, was about to disappear forever.

CHAPTER 14

TRAPPED

Alex lay curled in the corner of the abandoned trapper's cabin. The storm raged, piling snow higher and higher in the clearing. Alex lay on the hard floor, listening to the howling wind.

What am I going to do? No one even knows I'm here. But I'm the real Alex!

He looked out the broken window. A tear slid down his nose. He didn't really do anything terribly well or better than anyone else. He was shy. He was quiet. He was entirely forgettable, not the least bit memorable or important to anyone. No one would miss him.

He didn't even have a best friend.

Yes, you do! You have Needles!

Alex sat up. In all the weirdness of the past few hours, he had almost forgotten about her.

Then Alex remembered something that had been bothering him. At school, The Other Alex had said *Needles was fine.* But how? Was she still out there somewhere? Waiting for Alex to save her?

Alex stood up and slapped his hands against his chest to warm up.

There was no point dying of hunger or freezing to death. He had to take care of himself if he was going to get out of this. And if there was any way to get Needles back, somehow, he had to try.

First thing tomorrow, I need to find food. And warm clothes.

He looked around the barren cabin. It wasn't much, but it was home for now. *At least it's not leaking,* he thought with a sigh. He lay back down on the cold boards and closed his eyes.

The snow stopped at dawn. It piled up against the cabin in layers. Every bone in his body ached, but Alex got up. He rubbed his arms and legs to warm them. Then he crept through the snowy woods and hid at the edge of the forest.

Alex watched his house.

The kitchen door opened, and The Other Alex walked out into the snowy morning. Alex gasped. It was the strangest sensation, watching someone else being you.

The Other Alex had a backpack, a sleeping bag, a pillow. He was going to another sleepover. The Other Alex hopped into the pickup truck.

A moment later Carl came out of the house with a tool box. He put it in the back of the truck, then he and The Other drove off.

Alex's house was empty.

The real Alex darted across the snowy yard, opened the back door, and stood in his quiet kitchen. His heart hammered in his chest, and the clock above the stove tick-tick-ticked away.

Weird that I feel like a thief in my own house.

He ran up to his bedroom. The Other Alex had made himself at home.

"He wore my pajamas!" Alex made a mental note never to wear that pair again. He grabbed a backpack, two huge sweaters, clean jeans, another T-shirt. Dry socks. His prized binoculars. He ran into the bathroom and grabbed his toothbrush, hoping The Other hadn't used that, too — *gross!* — then slipped downstairs.

He opened the pantry door and stuffed cans of beans and soup into his backpack. He grabbed bottled water, orange juice, a small bag of apples. He made himself toast and peanut butter for breakfast and drank two glasses of apple juice. He was so happy to eat, to be warm, at least for a moment.

Then he stood at the top of the basement stairs.

He needed a sleeping bag and they were in the dark basement. He hesitated …

… *WHAT'S THAT?*

A pickup truck pulled into the driveway! He peeked out the kitchen window and saw Carl get out of his truck. He'd dropped off The Other Alex and was already back!

There was no way out!

Alex tiptoed as quickly as he could down the basement stairs in the dark. He stood at the bottom, clutching his backpack, then hid behind the furnace.

Carl came into the house, whistling. Alex heard him drop his keys onto the kitchen table. Carl opened the fridge. Whistled some more.

Then Carl turned on the basement light.

Then Carl started slowly down the stairs.

Whistling.

Alex stood frozen behind the furnace. He peeked for a second and saw Carl holding the heavy tool box.

Don't find me. Don't find me. Don't find me. Stop whistling. Don't find me.

Carl stopped at the bottom of the stairs. He cocked his head. He stopped whistling. He clutched the tool box. He listened.

Then he slowly turned and walked toward the furnace …

… *Ding-dong!*

The back doorbell rang.

"Hmph," Carl said. He paused.

Ding-dong! The doorbell rang again.

Carl turned away from the furnace. He put the tool box on his workbench. Then he slowly climbed the stairs, whistling, and turned out the basement light.

Alex heard his brother open the back door.

"Yes?" Carl said to someone outside.

A strange voice said something that Alex couldn't hear. But the voice was weirdly familiar. He'd definitely heard that raspy, squealy voice before!

The two tall strangers!

Carl said something in reply then shut the door. He stomped across the kitchen and up the stairs to the second floor. A few moments later, Alex heard the upstairs water turn on. Carl had gone upstairs for a shower!

Alex grabbed a sleeping bag, then he slipped up the basement stairs and out the back door.

He ran across the yard, through the woods to the cabin. He was in such a hurry, he didn't notice the two tall strangers in overcoats and sunglasses hiding at the edge of the barn.

Watching.

CHAPTER 15

SNOWSHOES AND SLEIGH BELLS

It was a long, cold weekend.

With the sleeping bag and dry clothes, Alex didn't freeze. With the food, he didn't starve. He wasn't exactly comfortable, but he was still there.

Still the real Alex.

He had to think. He had to plan. But nothing came to him. How do you plan for something like this? A weird evil twin that turns up and replaces you?

He *couldn't* vanish forever, though. He couldn't allow himself to disappear. Needles might still be out there, and she needed him.

On Sunday afternoon, Alex crept out of the cabin. It had snowed more in the night, and now the snow was too deep to walk through. He stepped off the cabin porch and fell into snow up to his hip.

There were snowshoes in the barn.

He had to get them. So he struggled as quietly as he could through the woods back to his house. He stopped at the paddock and watched.

Carl's pickup truck was gone.

Alex raced across the yard to the barn. He snuck inside and ran to the tack room. There was a sleigh for the horses, which they hadn't used in years. There were old saddles and riding equipment and a box of tools and horseshoes.

A rack of old cross-country skis and snowshoes lined the wall. He reached up and pulled a smaller pair of snowshoes off a hook. He slung them over his shoulder and peeked in on Pins. He walked toward her, holding out his gloved hand.

She snorted and backed up in her stall. He moved closer.

"What's wrong, Pins?" But the horse kept her distance. Alex moved a little closer, and she tossed her head and stamped her hoof. A warning: *Keep away.*

"Don't you know me? It's me, Alex!" But Pins did NOT know him. She didn't know him at all. She snorted, tossed her head, and kicked the stall.

"SHHH! SHHH, Pins. It's ME! Alex!" he whispered, but the horse kicked and snorted until he had no choice. He had to leave. As soon as he was gone, Pins settled down.

She doesn't know me!

Alex darted across the yard, back to the edge of the woods. As he strapped on the snowshoes, a pickup truck pulled into the yard. He crouched behind a tree and watched.

Carl and The Other Alex got out.

"I can't wait!" The Other Alex said.

"Okay, let's go," Carl answered. They walked into the barn. Alex-waiting-in-the-woods heard horses, voices, something big moving around.

What could that be?

Then the sleigh moved into the sunshine, with Pins and Minnie in the harness! Carl and The Other Alex sat in the high seat, covered by a bright red blanket. Carl handed the reins to The Other, then Carl and The Other Alex rode off into the snowy afternoon, the bells on the sleigh jingling softly.

I've never even been on that sleigh before!

With a bitter heart, the real Alex, the cold, scared, and hungry Alex, headed back into the woods, alone.

CHAPTER 16

MIRROR, MIRROR

Alex hid behind bushes at the side of the school. His snowshoes leaned against the window to the boy's bathroom — *his* bathroom. It was Monday morning, and he'd woken up with the sun, then hiked through the snowy fields to school.

He finally had a plan.

The school bus — *his* school bus — pulled up, and a group of kids piled out, laughing and talking.

And *he* was in the middle of them. Or The Other Alex was, anyway.

The Other Alex walked into the school, surrounded by friends that the real Alex *never* had. Alex watched as his evil twin bragged to the other kids about the two sleepovers that weekend.

I don't brag, the real Alex thought bitterly from his hiding spot.

Then everyone was inside the school and the bell rang. Alex looked around. The coast was clear. He slipped in the back door. He walked quickly along the halls.

A few teachers walked past, but no one saw him.

Alex heard a basketball game going on in the gym. He crept to the door, and peeked in …

… just in time to see The Other Alex score a three-point shot that made everyone stop. Then the team ran over and high-fived The Other Alex.

He really is amazing at basketball. Or is it me who's amazing at basketball? Is he only good at it because I am?

The real Alex felt dizzy. It was so strange to see himself playing basketball that he had to turn away. He couldn't think about it too hard or he might lose sight of what he was doing. Why he was there. He slipped past the principal's office, then past the lunchroom and down the stairs to the basement.

As he'd lain in the cabin the night before, he had realized he had to talk to someone. He couldn't do this alone, and the only — well not person exactly, but *voice* — that had made any sense in the past few days was his reflection in the bathroom mirror.

Not much to go on, he knew. But he had to start somewhere.

He stepped into the technically off-limits boy's bathroom.

Empty.

I'm sneaking into my school to talk to myself. To try to figure out how to stop my evil twin from taking over my life. Even I can see how crazy this is. So ... does that mean I'm not crazy? If what I'm doing seems crazy?

He stood in front of the mirror and looked at himself. He really didn't look too good. He was dirty, for one thing. The cabin didn't exactly have a shower in it. And he looked thin and dark, like a wild dog.

But there was something more. He almost looked like he wasn't really there. He looked flimsy. Missing in action.

He took a deep breath. And spoke to the boy looking back at him.

"Hey. Alex. Um. It's *me*. I'm wondering if you can give me some advice?"

His own face looked back at him. He stuck out his tongue, and his reflection did the same thing. He made a face. So did his reflection. He winked at himself.

His reflection winked back.

"Are you still in there, Alex?" he asked. His voice was shaky. He was so tired. And cold. And he really felt ... alone. And scared. Definitely scared.

What if he really was disappearing for good? Both outside and inside the mirror?

"I hope so, because I really need you right now. I can't tell anyone else what's going on, it's too crazy. I'm not even sure what's real and what isn't. Please be in there." Alex stared at the boy's face in the mirror. His face.

"If you're not in there, then I have no one left to talk to." Alex looked at his sad face ...

... then the boy in the mirror grinned.

"Well, talking to yourself definitely isn't a great sign," his reflection teased. "But asking yourself if you're crazy probably is. Would a truly crazy person ask if he was crazy?" Alex stared at himself, and his reflection crossed his arms.

"Get a grip, Alex. Yes, I'm still in here. Who else would be reflecting back at you in a mirror? So, you're wondering what you should do to get your life back, is that it?" Alex-outside-the-mirror nodded. He'd never felt so mixed up. Or so alone.

"What am I going to do?" he asked himself.

Alex's reflection was much wiser and calmer than he was. If that was even possible.

Which it really wasn't.

"Well, I'd like to say that I'll come to the rescue, but I'm just a reflection. I'm afraid you'll have to save us," Alex-inside-the-mirror said.

"Obviously," Alex answered himself.

"But I CAN tell you something that you need to hear," his reflection added.

"Okay, what? Get to the point, would you?" Alex-outside-the-mirror was losing patience. He was tired, hungry, cold, and all alone in the world. Plus he was talking to himself in a haunted mirror.

Not one of those things was terribly pleasant. His reflection pulled up close to him, nose-to-nose on the other side of the glass.

"You need help, Alex. You have to trust someone and tell them what's happening," his reflection whispered.

"I came all this way, on SNOWSHOES, for you to tell me THAT?" Alex was getting mad. "I know that! Why do you think I'm here talking to you! Even if you ARE in a haunted mirror!" he shouted. His reflection raised his eyebrows.

"Haunted? Really? Is THAT what people say about it?"

Alex-outside-the-mirror nodded. "Yes. Well … is it?"

Alex-inside-the-mirror laughed. "I'm pretty sure it's just me in here! At least no one else has turned up yet. I'll let you know if anyone does, though!" His reflection rolled his eyes and smiled. He looked so brave. So wise. Alex wondered if he could ever look like that.

But he's me, really. Isn't he?

His reflection went on. "Look, kid-with-an-evil-twin, you're losing the battle here. The Other Alex is now basically you. He's up there with your face and body, playing basketball with *your* name. He's living in *your* house. Your family think he's *you*. Even your horse doesn't know who you are anymore. You can't do this alone. Tell someone. But tell the RIGHT someone. You already tried your classmates, your teachers, Dr. Philips, and Mrs. Finkman, and you know how well that turned out."

His reflection looked cleaner than Alex-outside-the-mirror. And more confident. Better fed. Happier somehow. Which was annoying.

"So who has offered to help you? Anyone come to mind?" His reflection looked at his fingernails and brushed them on his chest.

Alex thought. The words "Boy Who Is Known as Alex" popped into his head. In a strange, piggy voice.

"Only one person. Well, two, I guess. If they *are* people. Which I'm not sure about. I'm not even sure they're real or if I imagined them."

His reflection pointed a finger at him. "Am I real? But you're still here talking to me, aren't you? You have to get help where it's offered *sometimes*, Alex, my friend. Just pick wisely. And don't stop asking for help until someone actually *helps* you. That's my advice for the day. Good luck!" Then his reflection winked at him.

And stuck out his tongue.

The next second Alex was looking at himself again. His tear-stained, dirty, frightened face. But there was something different about him, too.

There was a wise voice in the mirror and in his head.

And it seemed to know what to do.

Alex was about to say goodbye when the bathroom door opened. Alex almost jumped out of his skin. The young janitor's friendly face appeared.

"You know, you probably shouldn't talk to yourself all alone in a haunted bathroom mirror. Not a great idea," the janitor said pleasantly. "People will begin to worry about you." He propped the bathroom door open with his foot. He took a long look at Alex.

"Are you okay, kid? You really look …"

Please don't say invisible.…

"… like you could use a friend. And don't tell me you weren't talking to yourself in here, because I heard you. Unless, of course, your reflection is talking to you." The janitor rubbed his hand on his coveralls.

"Name's Jim. What's yours?" Jim held Alex's gaze and offered his hand. There was nothing Alex could do but shake it.

"Alex," he mumbled. He looked at Jim. No glowing-green-goo eyes, just nice brown ones. After the fear and isolation of the past few days, shaking Jim's warm hand felt almost too normal. Like Alex had no right to be doing it.

"Nice to meet you, Alex. Now out you go!" Jim shooed Alex out of the bathroom. He watched the boy disappear down the hall.

"That boy really does need a friend," the janitor said to himself. Then he went back to his mop and bucket.

CHAPTER 17

PIG WHO IS
KNOWN AS BELLA

oonlight pierced the clouds and shone on the floor of the cabin. Alex stared out the window at the bright silver sky.

His reflection had said, *Tell someone. But tell the RIGHT someone.*

Great advice, he thought. *But who's that?*

Mr. Timbert, Mrs. Finkman, Dr. Philips, his brother, his mother, his father, his classmates, even the lady in the principal's office. No one could help him.

He looked at the dark night, the silver stars. He'd never felt so alone.

Suddenly a green light flashed outside in the sky. Then disappeared!

What's that?

Alex ran outside. The silver moon shone on the snow and the stars burned bright in the dark winter sky. He turned his binoculars to the heavens, scanned left, then right, then zipped his binoculars back to the right again. There.

The green light again!

A green, misty light formed and swirled gently above the trees near McGregor's farm.

He looked for a long time. The smoke — or whatever it was — was definitely there. And it was *green*.

Everything had started with the green goo in the clearing the night that Needles vanished. The strangers had stood in a weird green swirling smoke. Or was it fog? Carl's photocopy of the newspaper from Mrs. Cody talked about green fog patches in 1907.

And here was a swirly green mist.

Alex looked a moment longer, then made up his mind. He slipped into his snowshoes and crept across the clearing. The moon turned the field and forest silver and black, casting a perfect shadow of the boy sneaking along. Alex raised his binoculars, spying the trees above the McGregor farm in the distance.

The green fog came and went. He tried not to think about tall strangers in overcoats.

Or The Other.

Alex got closer to the McGregor farm. At the edge of the forest, he was wary, quiet, willing his snowshoes to fall softly. A strange wind waved the tree branches and danced snow all around him. He crept around the barn and heard the old horse shift uneasily inside. The McGregor farmhouse was dark. Alex stopped, hidden in the shadows.

And watched.

The green fog came from the pig shed. Across the barnyard he could see a large pig, out of the wind, curled up and cozy in her straw bed. A brand new fence bristled in front of her. *That's what Carl must have been doing, helping Mr. McGregor build the fence*, Alex thought.

The fog swirled and grew around the pig, then fell away. Then grew again.

In the darkness and shadow at the edge of the pig shed, a movement. A tall, dark figure reached up and adjusted sunglasses. Another tall, dark figure stood motionless beside it.

A weird, raspy voice came from the darkness.

"Pig Who Is Known as Bella, have you seen The Other?" the strange voice said. Alex tried not to gasp.

A grunting, squealing voice answered, "You ask that night after night. You know that I haven't." It came from McGregor's old sow, the mother pig to all the piglets in the pen. Alex stared in horror. The hair on the back of his neck slowly stood straight up.

Did that pig really just say that?

"Pig Who Is Known as Bella, we must find The Other," the second voice said. The green fog rose above the shed and into the trees whenever anyone, or any*thing,* spoke.

Pig Who Is Known as Bella snorted. "I haven't seen her — The Other, if that's what you're calling her — since she fell from the sky and crashed into the woods the day you all arrived." Behind the barn, Alex opened and closed his eyes, shook his head. He pinched his arm as hard as he could. He bit his lip until it hurt.

Somehow, weird just got weirder.

Fell from the sky?

"Pig Who Is Known as Bella, we must find The Other." The tall figures swayed by the pig

shed, hands jammed deeply into overcoat pockets. The green fog swirled. The moon shone down on the weird scene.

The pig grunted. Then her voice got especially squealy. "IF I see this *Other* creature, of course I'll tell you. I do WANT my piglets back, you know. My poor babies. You *stole* them to turn into whatever it is you are." The tall strangers shuffled in the barnyard.

Clip clop. Their feet — hooves? — clattered on the icy ground.

"Borrowed, Pig Who Is Known as Bella. We borrowed their bodies to take this form. Your piglets are fine. We will return them unharmed when we capture The Other."

The old sow curled deeper into her straw, her remaining mostly grown piglets huddled close to their warm mother. "I do hope so," she snorted. "But you *really* should have asked."

Alex slowly lowered his binoculars. The moon broke through clouds and shone down on the pig shed.

"No wonder you can't find this *Other*. You're not very observant, are you?" she said a moment later. "There's a boy hiding over there beside the barn."

Alex gasped.

The pig and her piglets, the strangers, all turned slowly and looked at him.

The first stranger snatched off its sunglasses.

Green rays shot from the stranger's eyes and raced across the barnyard toward Alex.

Alex was too scared to move.

Squealed words rasped into the night: *"Are you The Other?"*

The green ray wrapped firmly around Alex like a giant squid tentacle. It held him and plucked him up into the air. Alex didn't struggle.

Why struggle? What was the point?

The green ray gently carried Alex across the barnyard and placed him on the ground in front of the pigpen. Then the stranger put the sunglasses on again, and the green ray vanished. The fog blew around them, the moon shone, and all was silence.

The pig, her piglets, and the tall strangers looked at Alex. He looked back at them and thought, *This would be difficult to describe to anyone. Even if I wanted to. Which I don't. And I hope I never do.*

What did it matter, anyway, what happened to him? He couldn't be in any more trouble than he was now. His evil twin, The Other,

had taken over his life. If his only hope was weird, much-too-tall-strangers with green eye-rays and a talking pig, he'd have to accept it. His reflection in the bathroom mirror had told him that much.

Mrs. Finkman's face flashed into his mind for a moment, too. "Let them help you," she'd said at the pharmacy door. He suddenly realized she might have actually meant it.

He took a long, steadying breath. Then he spoke.

"I'm not The Other. I'm Alex. The *real* Alex." The wind whistled past, the green fog blew. The assembled creatures, earthly and otherwise, stared at him. He went on....

"But I DO know where The Other is. And ... I need your help."

CHAPTER 18

ALEX-THE-(CREEPY)-AMAZING

I'm a hero!

Alex strutted down the hallway. Students high-fived him. Teachers high-fived him. Even the principal stopped to adore him.

"Well done, Alex. You've made Rosewood Public School very proud today," he said. And high-fived him. Alex nodded and smiled, taking it all in stride.

Everyone loved him, and why shouldn't they?

Their school won the basketball tournament because of *him*.

And that meant their school was hosting the quarter-finals the next day. If they won that, they went on to the semifinals, then who knew how far they could go? They could win the division!

Alex strolled into music class and sat at the drums. The day before, the teacher had decided that Bertram (Ram for short) wasn't as good as Alex at the drums. Ram stood at the triangle and looked sad.

Everyone told Alex he was great.

And, like most imposters, he believed them.

In fact, his greatness blinded him.

Which was why, as he played the drums, he didn't notice the almost-invisible boy that looked exactly like him creep past the open door of the music room. He didn't see the invisible boy stop across the hall in front of his locker and pull a note out of his coat. Alex-the-(Creepy)-Amazing didn't see the boy open the locker and put the note inside. He didn't see the invisible boy slide away, back out into the snowy day.

No, Alex-the-(Creepy)-Amazing didn't see any of that. He saw only adoring fans as they listened to him play the drums. Because on top of everything else that made him *so* amazing, he was also a rock star. Everyone said so.

After music class, Alex-the-(Creepy)-Amazing high-fived his way to his locker. He stopped, opened it ... and a note fluttered to his feet.

He read it: *If you want to see how great you can REALLY be, meet me in the haunted bathroom at lunch tomorrow.*

There was no signature. He frowned, stuck the note in his pocket, closed his locker, and walked down the hall.

More people adored him, calling out congratulations.

And they were right to. He was *so* great.

When Alex-the-(Creepy)-Amazing went outside, Carl was waiting in his pickup truck.

"Hey, Alex! Way to go! I heard about the basketball tournament," Carl said as his little brother got in the truck.

"Yeah, I'm pretty great. What's for dinner?"

"Oh, your favourite, of course. Whatever you want."

"What's my favourite dinner, Carl?" Alex-the-(Creepy)-Amazing looked at his brother and watched Carl's eyes turn bright green. Just for a second.

"Your favourite dinner is ... I can't

pronounce it." Carl looked puzzled. And his little brother smiled. A nasty smile, too.

"Don't worry, big brother, I can tell you how to make it. It's kind of a specialty, not from around here." Alex-the-(Creepy)-Amazing looked out the window. He sighed. It was all too easy. Carl was so simple — it wasn't hard to get his older brother to think and do whatever he wanted.

His mother and father might be a bit harder to train, though, whenever they returned from Australia, or wherever it was. But they'd come around.

He was thinking about all the things he was going to do in the coming days. Riding, teaching Carl how to make his favourite food, charming everyone at school, playing the drums, being the captain of the Rosewood Public School basketball team.

It wasn't that hard to hide in this body, in this life. It was easy.

Almost too easy, in fact. Practically dull. This boy, this town, this school. Not much of a challenge at all.

Alex-the-(Creepy)-Amazing sighed. It was almost boring to be so amazing.

And there was no one to stop him.

CHAPTER 19

A REAL REFLECTION

The next day, the real Alex stood in the haunted bathroom.

It was lunch. High noon. Showtime.

He clutched the sink and stared into the mirror. But the only person looking back at him … was him.

"Are you in there?" he whispered. But his own face whispered back. His smart, confident reflection wasn't in there.

"Come on, quit it. I need you here, now!" Alex was desperate. The Other Alex was going to turn up any second. And his reflection was just him. Shy, quiet, and invisible *him*. He was about to shout at himself when the door opened.

The Other Alex walked into the bathroom.

He looked cheerful. He looked confident. He looked like the real Alex, only much better. Clean and fed, for one thing. He wore a Rosewood Public School purple basketball jersey and gym shorts. A dark green "C" was stitched to the chest.

The "C" was for Captain.

"Oh, honestly, are you still here?" The Other Alex said when he saw the real Alex standing there. He looked genuinely annoyed. "I thought you disappeared days ago," he added.

The real Alex couldn't help feeling grubby and powerless next to The Other Alex.

But I'm NOT powerless, he thought. *The tall strangers told me what to do. I can do this. I wish my reflection was here to help, though.*

He took a deep breath.

"I'm still here," the real Alex said quietly.

The Other Alex looked bored and crossed his arms. "Well, you won't be here much longer. You've faded to practically nothing. Just look at you," The Other Alex said with a nasty smile.

I never smiled like that, Alex thought. *I'm much nicer than you are.*

"You haven't won," the real Alex said quietly. His heart pounded, and he was sure that he sounded puny and scared.

The Other Alex grinned that nasty smile. "Look, Mr. Invisible, I have a basketball tournament to win this afternoon. Why don't you just fade away now, like you're supposed to? No one cares about you."

Alex looked at his evil twin, so self-assured. He wanted just a tiny bit of that self-assurance. Maybe without the nastiness, though.

He thought about the tall strangers. They were counting on him. He thought about his horse, his beautiful cat, even his mother and father and Carl. They were worth fighting for, too.

"I'm not invisible. I'm right here. And I want my life back." Alex took a step toward The Other Alex.

"Don't come any closer," The Other warned. "Remember what happened last time? You don't want another burn, do you?"

Then it happened.

"You're a fraud, my friend," came a strong voice from the mirror.

Alex's reflection sprang to life, pointing one finger out of the mirror at The Other. "You're a fake," Alex's reflection said. "You're not really us. Why don't you come over to the mirror and show yourself. Show us who you really are?" he taunted.

The real Alex had the strangest feeling. Here he was, face to face with himself. Twice.

On his left was The Other Alex, in basketball shorts and a team jersey.

And on his right was his reflection, being brave in the mirror.

And somewhere between them was him. The *real* him. Whoever *that* was.

If this is what it's like to be a triplet, count me out, thought Alex (the real one, and possibly his reflection, too).

"Come over to the mirror, show us who you really are," his reflection taunted again.

But The Other Alex didn't budge.

"I've won. You've lost. Now I have to go, people are waiting for me."

The Other moved toward the door. It was now or never.

The real Alex pounced. He grabbed The Other Alex by the arm. His hand was on fire where he grabbed his evil twin, but he didn't care. He held on, and The Other turned to fight.

There was no being invisible now.

"No one even sees you! I'm better than you in every way!" The Other Alex shrieked. He tried to pull away, but Alex (the real one), dragged his evil twin in front of the mirror …

… and tried not to faint.

The *thing* in the mirror! The Other's reflection!

The real Alex would never forget it, not for as long as he lived. Two huge green eyes popped out above a slash of dark mouth. Long arms ended in white, fingerless blobs. Long legs stood on fleshless, rootlike toes.

The Other Alex wasn't Alex at all.

The Other Alex *wasn't even human*.

The real Alex held on tight while his evil twin shrieked, and squirmed, and moaned in the mirror. Alex's reflection looked suitably horrified. He shouted encouragement from inside the mirror.

"Don't let go! Hold him, Alex!"

"The strangers told me what you really are," Alex said, straining to hold The Other steady in front of the mirror. "You're an escaped criminal, a creature from another place, an …

alien! That burned green blob in the clearing, the day this all started? That was your ship! The tall strangers tried to catch you, but you crashed there and escaped."

The Other moaned and wriggled in Alex's grip. "And you're nothing like me," the real Alex went on. "You're cruel, heartless, even your smile is nasty. You don't have my thoughts, my kindness, you don't know what I'm thinking. You're nothing but a fake!" He was shouting now.

"I'm the REAL ME!" Alex yelled.

The Other squirmed and moaned. As Alex held on, his hands on fire, it finally came to him. What The Other Alex could never take from him.

The thing that made him ... *him*. *His* unique thoughts. Whatever *he* thought each moment, however he looked at the world, it was HIS way of thinking. HIS way of looking. He loved the snow. He loved the forest. He loved basketball, and math, and horses.

And Needles.

Even if he was a lonely boy, with only a cat for a best friend, the evil twin couldn't be inside his head.

Or his heart.

"You'll never be me," Alex whispered.

Alex held the creature in front of the mirror. It wasn't easy. The Other wanted to live.

But so did Alex.

Just a little longer. One full minute. That's what the tall strangers had said: *Hold The Other in front of the mirror for one full minute....*

"You can go now," the real Alex whispered. Tears streamed down his face, and his hands were blistered. He was going to die of the pain.

Suddenly the real Alex held on to ... air. On to nothing.

What the heck?

The purple basketball jersey lay on the floor. Empty.

No, not empty.

There on the tile floor, beside the basketball trunks and jersey, lay a small, twisted creature. A blob of green and white that grew and shrank, like a heartbeat. Two green eyes bulged out at the side of the blob, and it looked more like a deep-sea creature — a squid maybe — than a scary evil twin.

Alex's reflection came close to the mirror and peeked down at the pulsing thing on the floor. "You did it," Alex's reflection whispered.

The thing on the floor writhed and jerked, then lay still.

"You killed The Other," Alex's reflection whispered, impressed. Alex shook his head.

"No, it's not dead. The tall strangers said it's just dormant, sleeping, but not for long."

"What should we do with it?" his reflection asked.

Alex pulled an empty sandwich bag from his backpack. He gingerly reached down and picked the blob off the floor, careful not to let any of it touch him.

"Gross," Alex breathed.

"No kidding," his reflection added.

Alex zipped the sandwich bag closed and carefully put it in his backpack. The Other, in its real form, looked and felt exactly like a bag of slimy noodles. The tall strangers wanted what was left of The Other, even if it was just sleeping, and they wanted it fast, that night. Alex didn't ask why.

But he had no idea it would be so revolting.

Alex looked at himself in the mirror. He and his reflection.

The boy winked at him.

Alex was about to say something else, *thank you* probably, but the bathroom door burst open. Jim the janitor stuck his head in the room.

"There you are! The whole school is looking for you, Alex! They need their captain for the basketball tournament! Shouldn't you be going?"

Alex looked at the janitor for a moment, then at his reflection (who was doing a very good impression of being just a reflection). Alex reached down and picked up the basketball jersey from the floor. He looked at it, then slowly nodded.

"Yes. Yes, I guess I should," he said quietly.

Jim watched Alex run up the stairs, two at a time. Then the kind janitor turned and mopped the bathroom floor, which for some reason needed a good cleaning.

CHAPTER 20

THE GIFT

Alex stood in the cold early evening. The sun was going down over the treetops.

His basketball team won the quarter-finals. His teammates high-fived him and told him he was the best captain they ever had. He got invited for dinner at three different places, but he smiled, thanked everyone, and walked home.

He could get used to being popular tomorrow.

He still had the disgusting sandwich bag with his sleeping evil twin in his backpack. He felt queasy knowing it was there. He couldn't wait to get rid of it.

The tall strangers wanted him to bring it to the clearing.

He was here.

But where were they?

Low sunlight slanted across the trees, turning the snow orange and yellow. A blue jay called from the woods, the very first hint of spring, which was still a long way off. But it was coming.

Then a movement. The two tall strangers stood at the edge of the woods.

"Boy Who Is Known as Alex," came the squealed voice.

"I'm here," Alex answered.

"The Other, Boy Who Is Known as Alex. Put it on the snow." Alex unzipped his backpack and placed the sandwich bag with what was left of his evil twin on the snow. He backed away.

Gladly.

Suddenly, the green fog swirled around the strangers. Their long overcoats fell to the snow, and their sunglasses, too. Two squealing piglets appeared. They stared at Alex for a moment, then turned and trotted through the woods toward McGregor's farm.

Their mother, Bella, would be very happy to see them.

Where the piglets had been stood two tall, skinny creatures. Their green eyes glowed at the side of their heads, and they nodded at Alex.

He heard a voice in his head. Not a raspy, squealing pig-voice this time. More like a musical note. Or the voice of a friend.

"This is what we really are, Boy Who Is Known as Alex. Thank you for helping us capture The Other. We have chased her, and others like her, across the galaxy to this planet many times. But she is the last of her kind. They won't trouble you again."

"We will not return," the second voice said.

"Never?" Alex said.

"Never. Never is a long time, even for us, Boy Who Is Known as Alex," came the voice.

Then the strangers wrapped their long arms around each other and slowly melted together. A green ball glowed at the edge of the forest, rose slowly above the trees, then shot into the dark sky.

In moments, the aliens were a speck among the stars.

Alex heard the voice in his head one last time.

"Enjoy your gift, Boy Who Is Known as Alex. She is only slightly changed. She will live a

long, long life, a life as long as yours. A helpful reminder, perhaps, of what matters most to you."

Alex turned around.

The sandwich bag containing his evil twin was gone. In its place stood a fluffy, beautiful, yellow-eyed cat, raising her tail to say hello.

CHAPTER 21

ALEX FOR REAL

You know the rest of the story, don't you?
Alex and Needles leapt and played in the snow. They batted snowflakes. They laughed a lot. How often do you get to see your best friend again, after you think she's gone for good?

Then they went to the barn and said hello to Pins.

Soon Carl had dinner ready and called Alex from the barn. The brothers ate delicious spaghetti and meatballs. (Alex didn't even care that dinner looked a lot like the contents of a certain sandwich bag he'd just got rid of. He gobbled it up, anyway.) Later, Alex talked to his parents, who were coming home early in a week. Then he went up to his room, tossed the pajamas that The Other had worn into the garbage … and started his new life.

As himself. The non-invisible, real Alex.

The next morning the school bus stopped for him.

School that day, and every day afterward, was better than ever. His teachers counted him for attendance and called on him in class. He read *The World Book of Cats*, which he found in his desk. His bean sprout was the biggest in the science classroom. He played on the basketball team and was the most generous and unselfish captain they'd ever had (even Mr. Timbert said so). When it came to music, Alex couldn't stand to watch Ram stand so sadly beside the triangle. So he and Ram shared the drums in music class.

And became friends.

More than that, though, kids noticed him. In the halls, in the lunchroom, in the playground. He got invited to parties and sleepovers. He was still a little shy, and all the attention took some getting used to, but it only made people like him more.

Some said he was nicer than ever.

It took a little while to accept that he was stepping into a new life. The life that The Other had made for him. But really, what choice did he have? He wasn't fake. He was the real Alex. It was *his* life, after all.

The Other had just made it a little bigger for him.

Better than all that, though, the first day and every day afterward, he got off the school bus, walked up the laneway, and stuck his head into the barn. Pins was in her stall, waiting. Alex ran his hand over his horse's nose and gave her an apple from his lunch. And Needles sat waiting for him on a straw bale, too. As soon as she saw him, the huge cat yawned, stretched, then trotted over to rub against Alex's legs.

"Pins and Needles and me, the three of us together again. No one will ever know the truth, though, will they?" Alex said one afternoon. He looked down at his beloved cat, and for a second, just a second, her eyes glowed *bright green*.

He scratched her behind the ears, and she purred. It was okay if a tiny bit of The Other lived on. If Alex ever worried about fading away, all he needed to do was look into a mirror at the boy looking back at him.

Or into the occasionally bright green eyes of his cat.

They reminded him of who he really was. Likable, kind, shy. Lover of cats and horses, a wonderful basketball captain, great at sharing the drums, a good friend, little brother, and son, plus a lot more.

He was the *real* Alex, that day and every day for the rest of his life.

And he was *anything* but invisible.

THIS PART IS (ALSO) MOSTLY TRUE

Welcome to the end of the story, and if you've made it this far, congratulations! I told you at the beginning that it was scary and more than a little weird, and yet here you are. I bet you'll never look at fog the same away again. Especially if there's even a hint of green around the edges. People with green eyes might be off your list for a while, too.

You'll probably never look at pigs quite the same way, either.

But I suspect you're asking yourself a few questions.

Such as what *was* all that with the pigs? Well, they *are* very smart creatures. I think it makes perfect sense that visiting aliens would borrow pig bodies to walk around in. I mean, if you even *believe* in aliens, that is. Besides, who knows what secrets lie in the heart of a pig? Maybe they enjoyed turning into slightly human creatures who walked on their hind legs and wandered around with sunglasses on. But really, next time the aliens *should* ask before they borrow a budy.

You might also be wondering who, or *what*, exactly, was The Other?

An alien outlaw, for one thing. A stealer of people's lives, a thief, an evil twin, a doppelgänger, call her what you will. She wasn't very nice about it, either. There are many ways to make someone feel small, or invisible, and she was good at it.

It takes a lot of self-esteem to stand up and say: I'm me. The *real* me.

I know who I am.

And what about the two tall strangers? Aliens? Yes. The good guys? Also, yes, although you didn't think so at first, I bet. Friends? Very definitely. You never know where you'll find friends, though, sometimes in the most unlikely of places.

You have to ask for help once in a while.

Sooner or later, everyone does. Just don't stop asking until you find the right people (or aliens) to help you.

Finally, though, you're likely wondering what *really* happened to Alex? Did an evil twin really try to steal his life? Did his teachers, classmates, Dr. Philips, his brother, and everyone else controlled by The Other really burn with bright green eyes?

Or was the whole *an-alien-stole-my-body* and *my-town-is-going-crazy* thing just him cracking under the pressure of his parents being away for so long?

Well, let's just say that we can all feel alone and different sometimes.

And if Alex learned anything, it's this: when all else fails, you can *always* count on the person you see in the mirror for sound advice.

It's a good place to start, anyway.

You might be interested to know that Alex became a wonderful farmer. He grew up, inherited the farm, and kept pigs. He also had lots of friends, including Bertram (Ram for short). They started a band together and filled the barn with music, which made all the animals very happy.

There are only two things that were a little odd about Alex as he grew up.

One: Every now and then, he'd look in the mirror for a long time. If he thought no one was around, you might even hear him talking to his reflection. He talked to his pigs from time to time, as well. As far as I know, no one ever heard them talk back.

Two: He never, EVER, went out on foggy nights. In fact, when the fog curled up around the house on cold, snowy nights, he would take to his bed and whisper, "Beware The Other! I won!"

They're troubling. They're bizarre.
And they JUST might be true …

Weird Stories Gone Wrong

BY PHILIPPA DOWDING
ILLUSTRATED BY SHAWNA DAIGLE

JAKE AND THE
GIANT HAND (2014)
The ghastly truth about
a giant hand …

MYLES AND THE
MONSTER OUTSIDE (2015)
A rainy night, a haunted highway,
a mysterious monster …

CARTER AND THE
CURIOUS MAZE (2016)
Are you brave enough to
enter the curious maze?
Not everyone comes out …

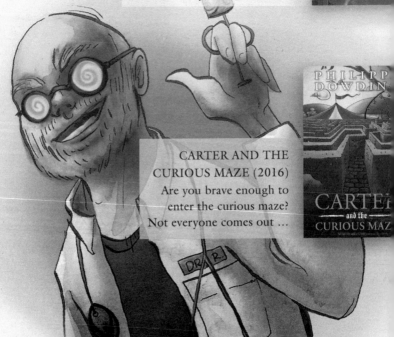

ALEX AND THE OTHER (2018)

An evil twin, a haunted mirror, and strangers who whisper … *BEWARE THE OTHER!*

BLACKWELLS AND THE BRINY DEEP (2018)

Shrieking mermaids, zombie pirates, an enchanted island, and *do you hear the distant drums?*

𝔚eird 𝔖tories 𝔊one 𝔚rong

IVE TREMENDOUSLY TERRIFYING TALES YOU'LL WANT TO SHARE WITH YOUR FRIENDS (SHOULD YOU WANT TO SCARE THEM SILLY).

#WeirdStoriesGoneWrong

More Books by Philippa Dowding

The Strange Gift of Gwendolyn Golden

Book 1 in the Night Flyer's Handbook series

This morning, I woke up on the ceiling …

So begins the strange story of Gwendolyn Golden. One perfectly ordinary day for no apparent reason, she wakes up floating around her room like one of her little brother's Batman balloons.

Puberty is weird enough. Everyone already thinks she's an oddball with anger issues because her father vanished in a mysterious storm one night when she was six. Then there are the mean, false rumours people are spreading about her at school. On top of all that, now she's a flying freak.

How can she tell her best friend or her mother? How can she live her life? After Gwendolyn almost meets disaster flying too high and too fast one night, help arrives from the most unexpected place. And stranger still? She's not alone.

Everton Miles Is Stranger Than Me

Book 2 in the Night Flyer's Handbook series

I wander around like any normal, paranoid, self-absorbed teenager. Do we all think we're being chased by deadly entities, I wonder? Probably, but how many of us actually are?

Gwendolyn Golden, Night Flyer, floats over the cornfields all summer. What draws her to the same spot, night after night? All she knows is that change is coming: she's starting high school *plus* there's a strange new boy in town.

He's Everton Miles and he's a Night Flyer, too.

Soon the mismatched teenagers face dangers they never imagined, including a fallen Spirit Flyer, kidnap, and the eternal darkness of The Shade. How will Gwendolyn handle her new life *and* grade nine? With help from The Night Flyer's Handbook and her strange new friend, it might not be that hard.

*CCBC's Best Books for Kids & Teens
(Spring 2017) Selection*